THE ONE WHO HOLDS THE LIFE

SRAVANI TALLAPURI

To Vamsee,

You are always there to hold my hand,

You are always there to support me,

You are always there to teach me,

You are always there to correct me,

You are always there to take care of me,

You are the light of my life.

Contents

Foreword

~~~Sudha Murthy Mam is always an inspiration to me to start writing a book.
~~~

Preface

I myself work as a Software Engineer in Bangalore. I always have a passion of writing a book after my academics, but never thought seriously about this. After marriage, my husband encouraged me to first read books . I selected fiction books and started reading them and slowly increased the interest on reading the books. Sometimes, i read the whole book overnight. There again, my passion of writing a book came into light. I was pregnant that time, so could not spend time in this area. During preganacy and with kids it went into dark again. Then again thought to write a book where i can share my preganancy experience to everyone. That is how it started.....

----Sravani

Curious, Fear, Restlessness

The little baby girl in the hands after 9 months of great wait. Still remember first 3 months of was a very horrible time and sweet period at the same time. No support from elders, only we two went thru that challenging time. Twice a day vomitings, could not eat at all, no tolerance to any food smell, no helper at home for taking care of house hold stuff. Was unable to sleep, eat, read, go to office. Early morning routine started with sickness, which may be nausea or actual vomiting, and does not just happen in the morning , the whole day. As it was for the first time, no idea was it ok or something wrong, when should we bother, when should not. Many questions with no answers.

Was working from home those days and things are manageable atleast from office end. Doctor Mahalakshmi never suggested any additional any additional tablet to stop vomtings apart from folic acid, Calcium and Iron through out preganacy. After completing third month and entering into fourth month things were back to normal. Vamsee was there for me always in all odds and evens.

Food cravings and aversions. The hormones changing in your body mean you will probably have heightened emotions, both positive and negative. And you will probably swing between these emotions.

Pregnancy might leave you feeling delighted, anxious, exhilarated and exhausted — sometimes all at once. Even if you're thrilled about being pregnant, a new baby adds emotional stress to your life.

It's natural to worry about your baby's health, your adjustment to parenthood and the financial demands of raising a child. If you're working, you might worry about how to balance the demands of family and career. You might also experience mood swings. What you're feeling is normal. Take care of yourself, and look to loved ones for understanding and encouragement.

CHAPTER TWO

Seemantham

Fourth month ended comfortably and fifth month started with active mood swings. Had to travel to hometown as we have ritual to perform called as Seemantham.

Brothers wife was also carring that time and she was in her ninth month. There is a saying in telugu no two preganant women should stay in same house at same time. So, could not go to my mothers place. On Novemeber 14th 2018 seemantham(it is a tradition to bless the preganant women with a healthy child and good health by giving her bangles, sweets, flowers) done. After that went to mothers house and stayed for two days. In those days one of my friend passed by taking too much of alochol. Sad news, which i heard those days.

It is quite common all these feelings during preganancy, women should go through all these days. You feel like eating/drinking something, but that smell or taste your stomach wont accept it, it is a real pain. Here in our case, everything has to be prepared by us and have to clean by us. The man behind my pain and gain is always my husband Vamsee. Without his support could not travelled this much with great memories during those day.

Returned back to banaglore in fifth month itself, the days were very good. Was going to office everyday in a separate cab provided by organization. I have three monkey friends where most of the office hours spent with them were crazy. Most of the time breakfast and lunch used to do in office itself. SAP is one of the best place to work for. It is not jsut saying, it is true, where anyone can feel it once you work here. We have a great flexibility, good policies, great vision and good work-life balance. Work was bit less those days and most of the time we spent in cafteria, chit chatting with friends. I used to drop my husband in the same company car while going to office and pick up in the same car while going back to home, as his office is on the way to mine. After reaching home, same small routine work cooking, cleaing utensilis, reading some books, sharing the day things with husband, walking, watching movies and so on,...It was a very relaxing period i can say.

CHAPTER THREE

Difficulties

I enjoyed preganancy during my sixth to Ninth month. It was normal, experiencing the baby kicks. The truth is that baby kicks are more like flutters at first, and you may not feel your baby move until halfway through pregnancy. But by the third trimester, your baby will be making some big moves that are impossible to ignore. It's important to keep in mind, though, that this is an average, and pregnancy weight gain varies from person to person and pregnancy to pregnancy.As you get closer and closer to delivery, your baby will begin to settle into your pelvis. As they move down, you may notice that your bump even begins to hang a little lower

I enjoyed outside food while eating, but the result was shown during night as too much of gasteric problem during night sleep and not able to sleep at all sometimes. There is one of the great book i read, named as SHUNYA and felt very nice book.

One more problem i experience during third trimester is never tightness in my leg. It was very painful, could not even move leg or uplift. Vamsee used to get up from his sleep and massaged my legs till the tightness get relieved. It was not great expereince i can say. Frequency of urination icreased like anything. Almost 7 to 8 times during night times and expereinced disturbance of sleep, but used to sleep during afternoon and hence not faced much difficulty

During my eight month was walking around the apartment and fell down on knees unexpectedly. No one was around to lift and myself got up and slowly reached our flat and sat on bed. I was bit worried if something would have happened to baby . There is an injury to my knee and elbow when there where light scratches and remembered the saying our elders used to say, if a mother fell down during preganancy some bad thing happen to the foetus in the womb and bit worried and slept thinking about it. After sometime my husband came from office and told him what happened and he consoled me and was fine after that. Things were smooth later.

CHAPTER FOUR

Calmness

Finally! After a long wait, due date is near. In the last month of pregnancy, and the baby will be arriving soon

Stopped going to office once enetered into ninth month. Before that was going twice a week or thrice a week. My mother, mother-in-law and sister-in-law came to bangalore to do seemantham in ninth month second time. It was on March 9th 2019, saturday. Invited near and dear ones and went well with beaautiful pictures and lots of memories. After that on next day, my mother-in-law and sister-in-law left to hometown as there was a wedding of our close relative and my mother stayed back with me, as she planned to stay with me till delivery. I got relived from project from March 11th 2019 and so no work and sit back and relax position till delivery. Was spending time with my mother, chit chatting with her and many more..

Tuesday morning went for regular check up and doctor told it will take some more time for delivery and real story started on the same day night.

CHAPTER FIVE

Delivery Date

Tuesday nigh around 9:30 we and my mother spoke with my younger sister over the phone and was lagughing, gossiping and spent well and went to bed to sleep. My husband was doing meditation and mother went to another room to sleep. I felt some water rushing out from urine passage after i lie down. Felt it could be white dischare and ignored it. Again the same thing happned and it was going continuosly without my notice. Called my mother and husband and by that time by nighty was fully drenched in that amonitic fluid and we rushed to hospital by booking OLA cab. Reached hospital aroun 10:30 PM and cab seat was also fully watered. Went to hospital and head nurse was there and she asked me to go for urine and come back that she want to test something below. Went to bathroom and observed that bleeding started. I was tensed and nervoused at the same time , holding husband hand tightly with tears in my eyes. He was calming down me and telling to me everything will be fine and things will be smooth. Night duty nurse took me inside and checked the baby position and some other tests she performed and called to the doctor and explained the situation. Doctor suggested to admit me in the hopsital and after 10 mins they gave us room. Amonitic fluid was passing continuosly. They changed my dress and passing my urine on the bed itself. Doctor came around 2:30 AM and checked my condition and told that i will get delivery by tomorrow and will try for normal delivery and left the hospital. The whole night was passing urine and amonitic fluid on the bed itself.

Morning around 7:30 AM doctor came and checked my condition again and informed the nurse to shift me to labour room. In the labour room i was accompanied with one nurse and was lying on bench. I told to nurse was feeling like passing urine. She allowed me once to go to bathroom, but could not go as i feel someone is stopping the passage of urine. Those hours were really painful. You cannot breathe, could not pass urine, could not sit, could not lie down. Pains has started and i was like the hell and by holding the nurse hand i was shouting like could not bear them.

Doctor entered the labour room around 10:30 and asked nurse to give some injection to me. Pains started frequently and was crying, shouting and so on.. Doctor asked my husband to go inside and give support to me. He came inside and by holding my hand he was telling dont worry, things are fine. I havent stopped crying, shouting and doctor came and asked him to leave the room. I was not leaving his hands and asking him to stay with me. Then she gave one more injection to my nerve and vomited everything what ever was there in my stomach and another injection. Pains started like hell. Both the legs were taken apart removing the clothes which were there on my bottom area. There were few guys as well and i did not felt shy on that condition as they are helping me to get another life into this world with me.

Doctor asked me to push the baby two times and baby will come out. There are two guys next to me on my upper side and doctor bottom side and two more guys next to her. There was one guy who kept hands on my stomach so that he could help me to push the baby from outer side. I took heavy breath and pushed the baby heavily for the first time and that person pushed the baby from out side by pushing with his hands. Then doctor asked to push heavily and baby will come out. I was crying, crying and telling her i was unable to do that and asked that helper will you please help me. Then, doctor said you do it from your end and he will help you. I took deep breathe and shouted SRI GANESHA and pushed harder same time, that helper as well. Heard my little one crying sound first time and its a baby GIRL. Doctor informed its a baby girl and time is 11.31 AM and now she named as "Vaaruni""

I was like quite silent as i dont have energy to talk as i shouted or cried like that. It was very lite and kind of relaxed position on bench. They took baby to give bath, they anstheia to sticth vagina as they cut it little bit to get the baby out. Felt bit painful, but compare to labour pains these pains were nothing.

They informed to my husband and mother that i was blessed with a baby girl and they showed me my little one and i saw her for the first time and kissed her on her chicks. That moment i forgot all the pain. pediatrician came and checked the baby and he told baby is healthy and some blood strains on her head while taking her out and changes are high for Jaundice. He informed to vamsee due to less space in mothers stomach, babys right leg was slightly not straight and asked to consult the Ortho.

After few mintues, nurse changed my dress and shifted me to the room on the wheel chair and baby was already in the room and surrouunded my nurses and they are calling her as PINKY PAPA as she was pinkish at that time. Vamsee was with mixed emotions. Tension-> Jaundice and leg foot issue and Happy-> for baby girl birth.

That is how my first baby saw the world on March 13th 2019, 11:31 AM with help of Dr. Mahalakshmi in the AAYUG Hospital, AECS layout, Bangalore.

CHAPTER SIX

Entry of Second one

It was around in the month of Janurary 2021, i missed my period and waited for few weeks before we went to hospiatal. That time i have particpated in AP elections and conveyed the news to my mother. But why i am in AP is another story. Let me tell that first. In 2019, covid19 started in India and was locked in Banaglore after our first baby 1st birthday. Lot many restrictions to travel or go outside. In Oct 2019, restrictions were removed and travelled to hometown to visit my brother-in-wedding . Offices were still closed and news like offices gets open only by 2021 end. So, thought to shift to hometown from banglaore by vacating the flat over there. Rented one small house in hometown near to my in laws house and in the month of November, shifted all the lauggaue to hometown .This is how the place changed from Bangalore to Proddatur, AP.

Tested Positive in the Month of January and convey the same news to family members. My mom-in-law was a kind of dilemma whether to show happy or unhappy face. But i decided to give birth to my second child. But the starting journey was not easy. My girl birthday was on March 13th, she is completing her 2nd year and entering into 3rd year. I went to order a cake for my little one and once i reach back home, noticed that bleeding started. I was full nervous and assumed that i lost my pregnancy and rushed to hospital. They did the scan and confirmed that baby is live and doctor suggested for bed rest for few days and gave injections for every 6 days. Bleeding is normal for some women and it stop in couple of days. But bleeding did not stop though 1 week completed. Many questions comes to your mind, whether the baby is ok or not, will it be healthy fetus or not, when will be the bleeding gets stop, is it ok to continue with this pregancy or should i go for abortion? Many more.. Those days were tough days. Thank God, he gave a best husband who was always with me in my odds and even.

Bleeding stopped after a week and was relaxed some what and continuing the injections as suggested by the doctor. I was in my 2 nd month that time. After few days, again the bleeding started. This time it was very heavy clots. Thought again my pregancy was gone and went for scan again. Heart beat is present and doctor told be on complete rest till you get 3rd month. It is only 10 days, i will be entering into 3rd month. But it will be difficult to be on rest with already on small kid to take care. Somehow managed, and enetered into my 3rd month and slowly bleeding stopped and did not faced this situation again till the delivery. Continued the injection till end of 4th month and stopped.

Covid 19, second wave started in the month of April and that time it was very severe and death rate also very high. Was going to hospital for normal check-up and taking that injection at home itself, as one of our relative is working as nurse and she used to give me that.

As usual, went for monthly check up and after that i got fever and body pains and gastric trouble. Thought it was a normal one and went to hospiatl and they gave some injection and came back home. But the sitaution is not normal, i was not keeping well at all. It was my 5th month and vomting started and very acidic. My husband and my girl was with me. One day, i still remember, ate watermelon and vomited everything in acidic form and he is next to me. My kid was very panic as she saw vomiting with louder sound and she is afraid. My mother came to see me and she decided to take me and my girl to home as i need some support. On the same day, my husband got fever and thought it was a normal one and i left to my mom's home. On that night, i was unable to breathe. Nose got blocked, can't sleep at all.

On the next day, my husband tested postive for COVID-19 and he informed me to get the test done even for me. Again, many things..if i test postive who will take care of kid, as death rate was high, do we recover or not? what will be the future. I informed my brother and he took me to hospital to do test for COVID.

Saturday morning, i feel very drowsy and feel like lying on bed. I ate idly, fed my daughter and was taking rest. I told to my girl that i am going to hospital to take an injection and will come back soon.

I left my girl in my mom's home and came to hospital. My fear came true, both me and my husband tested postive for COVID. Now, how about the kid? Doctor suggested to go for isolation and keep my girl away from us. She had light fever the day before we tested positive and i gave her paracetemol and she recovered. That was the first time i was away from her. She told me to come back soon while i was leaving to hospital and tears did not stop when i recall her. I asked my mother and brother to take care of kid for few days and they said ok.

Many things were running in mind like how i got affected with Covid? How did my husband got affected? Will the kid be ok in mother's home? Will she able to stay with out us? Will it have affect on my fetous?

My husband was waiting near the hospital and his condition was very bad. He has very high temperature and waited for few mins and they took my sample from mouth and result is "POSITIVE". They asked me to go for someother test and costed around rs. 4600/- and was waiting for reports. One of the nurse refered doctor SuryaPrakash Reddy as i was pregnant. I lost all the energy by waiting over there and had coconut water and sitting under the tree. Reports came and doctor gave few medicines as to start treatment for COVID.

Evening thought to go and check with SuryaPrakash as a second opinion. My brother took appointment and evening we went to hospital. My grandfather and brother were waiting infront of the hospital as the queue is very lengthy. After few mins, out turn came and he suggested few more medicines and he asked to keep kid away from us atlease for a week. My brother said he will keep her with him. We left back to home and it was isolation in the home. It was really hell.

CHAPTER SEVEN

Real Rush Started

After came back to home, was thinking how to handle the things. Me and my husband lying on the floor and thinking about my girl and the one in my stomach. That was the first time was awy from my kid. You never know how difficult it is to stay away from kid who is very small in age and very pampered girl. Tears, fear, angry, sad, many emotions...

On the next day, had breakfast, took tablets and called my mother and asked how is she? did she had food? is she crying? did she had bath? is she happy? is she playing well? like many questions and used to cry as i am in a situation where i have to keep my daughter away from me and was counting days.

Same night , fever started for my husband, high temperature 102 , 103 celesius. He was taking medicines, still the temperatures are not reducing. Whole night same condition, giving him cold bath with towel, checking the temperature , still fever not reduced. Next day morning vistied doctor and he suggested it will be same for few days, continue the same medicine and suggested to go for CT scan. As it was sunday, no hospitals to go for CT scan and thought to do the same on monday morning. Sympots were very severe for my husband. Full cough, high fever, unable to breathe properly, no stammina. But one relief, pulse is good. For me everything is fine, no symptoms were shown. Monday mroning scanning centers were busy, somehow got token and went overthere. My husband is unable to sit also for longer time, he feels always to sleep. Waiting time is high and he is unable to breathe properly. Some how he managed to get the scan done and found that virus ring near the chest. Doctor suggested other medicines from 8th day onwards. He was unable to go to bathroom as well, because of breathing problem. After 10th day, he regained strength and felt better. I was just praying to god to help us, that was the only hope.on 12th day, his covid test is negative and mine was still not negative. But were fine, no symptoms were shown and recovered fully. I was eager to go and meet my little girl .

After 15th day, i gave sample to test and went to meet my little girl. She hugged me as she saw me after many days. You can't express those feelings. Tears rolled in my eyes. I understood in that hug how much she missed me, how much she worried, how much pain she went thru. Prayed to god to never give this kind of situation to anyone. Let's end this kind of drama by now.

CHAPTER EIGHT

Days after Recovery

After staying in my mom's home for couple of days, i took my girl to my home as my husband's grandmother died because of covid. By that time, i am in my 6th month of preganacy. Blleding stopped, my little one is with me, husband recovered fully. Tension free mind.

Started back office work and normal check up's every month, enjoyed my days with little one, sleeping during office hours, days were smooth and went well.

When i entered into 9th month, there were some pains, unable to pass urine freely, tightness in the below stomach area, baby kick's. I was able to sit down without any issues. Body is flexible. Able to carry my little girl on my lap, used to go for walking everyday for 30 mins. It was smooth preganacy after enetring into 6th month and good old days.

CHAPTER NINE

Final Day with Second One

On october 19th 2021, i had egg bhurji for dinner and lying on bed , playing with my little girl. It was around 9PM and she jumped on bed and for that one jump amontic fluid started leaking and bleeding started. Informed my mom-in-law and rushed to hospital, keeping baby in my mom-in-laws home. In between called to my mom and told her the situation and she started to hospital.

There was only one duty nurse and she is very young and interested in speaking in phone. I told the whole situation and she informed the head nurse and asked us to wait. Later she asked us to go for covid test and the result was negative. Amontic fluid was releasing continuosly and just waiting for head nurse. She came and saw the whole situation and she told will give some injections and will do the delivery as fluid is going. She took me to labour room and gave injections and asked me to go room and wait till the labour pains get start. After that i felt droswy and about to fell. Nurse came and holded my hand, made me to sit on chair. After that i had vomited everything and shifted me to room.

Around 12 AM on October 20th 2021, pains started. My mom and sister informed the nurse and she shifted me to labour room. Agian they gave one more injection and doctor entered the labour room and pain started frequently which were unbearable. I was shouting shouting and they asked me to turn to ne side and asked me to push the baby. I was shouting like "Madhava Keshava" and pushed the baby and it's baby boy born at 12:21 AM Oct 20th 2021 who is now named as " Narasimha Aaditya". When he was born, it was raining very heavily, windy, dogs are shouting

Doctor informed to my elders and they shited me to room and real pain started now again.

Re-born

After shifted to room, pains started again near vagina which is abnormal. I informed my sister and nurse came and gave some injection and was telling it was paining very badly. Nurse told it is quite normal after delivery and she left room. My husband also left, as my little girl is at home waiting for him to sleep. I slept unconsciously. After an hour my sister came to me as i was sleeping without any complaints. I was shedded in blood unconsciously. Bleeding is going like water, full cot on blood. She rushed to head nurse and told the situation. She ranned to me and checked my pulse, it was down. She was shivered and shifted me to labour room . My nighty was full with blood . I don't remember any of these things. They changed my dress and shifted me to labour room. No blood in body, doctor also very afraid and they are rubbing my hands and she asked my sister to arrange for blood quickly. Everyone came to hospital and they started searching for blood.

I was unconscious, don't know what's happening, not responding to anyone. It was windy and raining very heavily at the same time. My brother-in-law and others were searching for blood. Doctor called my mother inside and explained her that i have two placenta and she told that she will remove them now. After the delivery, one placenta comes along with baby. Another one was there inside the stomach and it moved after the delivery. And it caused this much of bleeding and it was recognised for the correct time. She promised to my mom, that she will take care and arrange blood for her immediatley. One of our family member came to give blood in that time and they took for blood check and everything. It was mid night around 2 AM in the morning. It was raining, nurse informed other nurses also for blood as my situation is very serious. There was another male nurse, who rushed to hospital at that time and tried his best to know the situation and help us. Head nurse was still rubbing my hands and feet and trying to get me into conscious, but no luck. Doctor removed blood clots whatever was there and she asked to observe me. My sister, brother-in-law, everyone in the family searching for the blood. As it is the mid- night, it was difficult to get the blood of same group. Finally our family friend Srilatha came and gave blood and they started dripping it to me. My little one was crying for milk as he feels hungry as he came out of stomach. My mom fed him bottle milk and he was ok for that time.

After the blood was given to me, i came slowly into conscious. Was able to open the eyes and closing. Head nurse was still rubbing hands and praying to god, nothing should happen to me. She is slapping on my cheecks to open my eyes. I was slowly coming into consciousness and able to hear the voice of male nurse and head nurse, but not fully. After sometime, i am able to open eyes clearly, but not able to talk. Still, the bleeding was going. Head nurse asked me how am i and how am i feeling. Not able to talk. She thanked god and saw tears in her eyes and she kissed on my fore-head. They dripped another packet of blood and this whole process took whole night and around 5 AM i came into conscious. Nurse was there till that time and slept for sometime. Around 6 AM, i woke up by hearing my baby boy crying sound. And saw my mother-in-law next to me. I started talking and asking how are kids. I told her little one is crying, feed him some milk. She told my mom is taking care of her. After sometime, my sister-in-law came with my litle girl. My girl was sitting next to me and tears did not stop from eyes. With her little hands, she is cleaning my tears and saying don't cry ma, i am there for you. That moment is enough for me. She was my mother that time. My sister-in-law was telling , that my girl don't want to stay at home, she want to see me, so she brought her to hospital. She was asking why many bandages to my hand and all.She saw her brother and telling he is very cute. Then head nurse came and asked me how am i feeling and she explained the whole sitaution to me what happened in the night. I told her still bleeding is going like urine. They she asked my sister-in-law, daughter to leave room as she want to check. She checked and told doctor will come and examine . I was feeling trusty and asked for water. She told only drink little bit and my mother-in-law came and gave some water.

After sometime, doctor came and told they need to scan and check where are the clots still present. Male nurse kept me on wheel bed and took me to scanning room and he asked, whether i can walk till the inside of room. I said no, he only carried me on shoulder and kept on bed of scanning room. Then they scanned and found clots are still there and they said by laproscopy they remove the clots and everyting will be fine after.

They shifted me to operation theater and doctor told via laproscopy they will remove clots by giving ansthesia. I said ok, and they gave ansthesia to me. I don't remeber anything after that and came into conscious in the room after my sister-in-law slapping me on cheeks to wake me up. After sometime, i came to conscious and was able to see everyone and also my champ was looking at me with his big eyes open.

After a while, i was feeling ok, but still some pain is there. Breast fed my champ after sometime and things were falling ok.

Before the discharge, went to meet the doctor, she told it was very rare case and she saw this case 11 years ago. She told it all happened with two placenta and was recoginsed at correct time, otherwise i might have died my now and it is a "RE-BORN" for me. If the another placenta was not recognised and stayed in stomach, it must be serious sitaution to the mother. She told not to go for another pregancy and stop with 2 babies.

In the evening, discharged from hospital and came to home. This is story of "The one who hold the life". Hope you all re-called your delivery and preganacy experience. Do share your feedback/any suggestions/experiences @sravani.kushi@gmail.com, by keeping the book title as the subject.